# THUMBELINA

## Retold by Marianna Mayer
## Illustrated by John O'Brien

S0-BBE-728

### A Little Simon Book

Published by Simon & Schuster, Inc.
New York

Text copyright © 1986 by Marianna Mayer. Illustrations copyright © 1986 by John O'Brien. All rights reserved including the right of reproduction in whole or in part in any form. Published by LITTLE SIMON, A Division of Simon & Schuster, Inc. Simon & Schuster Building, Rockefeller Center, 1230 Avenue of the Americas, New York, New York 10020. LITTLE SIMON and colophon are trademarks of Simon & Schuster, Inc. Designed by Nina Tallarico. Manufactured in the United States of America. Also available in JULIAN MESSNER Library Edition.   1 2 3 4 5 6 7 8 9 10

**Library of Congress Cataloging-in-Publication Data** Mayer, Marianna. Thumbelina. Adapted from Hans Christian Andersen's Tommelise. Summary: A tiny girl no bigger than a thumb is stolen by a great, ugly toad, and subsequently has many adventures and makes many animal friends before finding the perfect mate in a warm and beautiful southern land.
  [1. Fairy tales]   I. O'Brien, John, 1953-ill.   II. Andersen, H. C. (Hans Christian), 1805-1875. Tommelise.   III. Title.
PZ8. M4514Th  1986   [Fic]   85-30258*        ISBN 0-671-62089-4 (lib. bdg.)        ISBN 0-671-62088-6

nce there was a woman who wished for a child of her own, but she feared she could never have one. In the hope of getting some advice, she went to visit an old witch. Fortunately, this particular witch wasn't the wicked sort but a good witch, who was much admired in the district for her healing potions and wonderful remedies.

When the woman explained what was in her heart, the old witch smiled and said, "I think I can help you, my dear. Just give me a moment." With that, the witch got up and went looking in a big wooden cupboard. Soon she returned and dropped a few seed kernels into the woman's hand, saying, "You must plant these at once."

"Why, they look like ordinary barley," remarked the woman.

"But they aren't!" declared the old witch with a jolly laugh. "And mind you don't let your chickens eat them, for that would be a terrible waste. You see, dear, these are *magic* kernels! Plant them carefully. A little flower pot should do nicely. Be sure to set the pot on the windowsill where it can catch the sunlight. Then water it once a day and I think you'll be pleased with the results."

"Thank you! Oh, thank you so much," said the woman as she hurried off.

For Nancy Hall
—M.M.

To Margie
—John

This Book
Belongs to:

Rachel P.

As soon as she arrived home, the woman carried out every step of the witch's instructions. She was quite prepared to wait a long time for the magic seeds to begin working, but the next morning, to her very great surprise, her efforts were rewarded. A beautiful flower, like a tightly closed tulip bud with red and yellow petals had already broken through the soil. The woman leaned down and gently kissed it, saying, "What a lovely blossom!"

At that moment the bud began to open slowly and there, at the very center, sat a tiny girl. When the woman saw the child she was filled with happiness.

"Oh, my dearest darling! I shall call you Thumbelina, for you are no bigger than my thumb." And this was true: the child was not much more than an inch tall.

Everything she might have wished for was given to her, yet Thumbelina never grew spoiled. Indeed, her temperment was as gentle and as sweet as she was beautiful.

There was a tiny bed made from a highly polished walnut shell for Thumbelina to sleep in. The bed was fitted with a mattress of white rose petals, a snug pillow of purple violets and a coverlet of Queen Anne's lace.

During the day, when the weather was fine, she played outside in the flower garden. There a plate filled with water and ringed with fresh flowers was her own private swimming pool. Sometimes Thumbelina set a tulip petal on the surface of the pool. Then, climbing onto the petal, she floated from one end of the pool to the other, using two blades of grass for oars.

One summer night, when the lights were out and the moon was full, Thumbelina lay in her tiny bed fast asleep. Silently, a great brown toad hopped onto the window ledge and slipped into the house through an open window. She was a nosy toad with big gloomy eyes that searched the room to see what there was to see. In no time, the toad spied Thumbelina asleep in her bed.

The toad drew closer and closer, until her large eyes stared right down on the lovely girl. "Here is the perfect wife for my son!" said the toad to no one in particular.

In a flash, she took up the walnut shell, pillow, mattress, child and coverlet and hopped away. The toad crept out the open window and fled into the flower garden without waking Thumbelina, who slept peacefully on and on.

A stream ran through the garden and along its marshy banks tall, thick reeds grew. It was here that the big brown toad lived with her dull-witted son. Both mother and son were most unpleasant creatures. Even other toads would have nothing to do with them.

When the toad-son saw Thumbelina sound asleep in her tiny bed, he stared down at her fixedly. Then he said at the top of his voice, "Croak! Croak!"

"Hush up, my precious! Or you shall wake your bride," whispered toad-mother. "We don't want her to escape. So be ever so quiet."

The toad-son shut his gaping mouth and nodded to his mother obediently.

"Now then," toad-mother continued in a harsh whisper. "I will put her on one of the water-lily pads out on the stream. She won't be able to run away from us there. In the meantime, I must ready your new home in the mud where you and your wife will live happily for ever and ever."

The water lilies had roots fixed deep down below the stream. But from the surface of the water the flat green leaves appeared to float free of root or stem. Toad-mother dove into the stream and swam

out with the walnut shell balanced upon her head. She looked from one broad lily pad to the next until she was satisfied that she had chosen the largest. Here, far away from land, she placed the walnut shell with the sleeping Thumbelina.

Quite early the next morning, Thumbelina awoke in her strange surroundings. The poor maiden was very frightened when she realized where she was, for the stream bank was far away. If she tried to swim such a long distance, surely she would drown.

With the new mud dwelling complete, toad-mother scrambled
back into the water to see to her captive. Toad-son dutifully followed and when they reached Thumbelina, he let out a loud
"Croak!" and grinned foolishly.

Toad-mother nodded her head with pride and said, "You, my girl,
have found yourself a most uncommon husband. Count yourself
lucky indeed that my son is willing to make you his wife. As if this
weren't enough, I've seen to your new abode. Every inch of it is
covered in mud, just the way my dear boy likes it. If you're a
good homemaker it will last you both a lifetime."

Thumbelina was speechless. She looked from toad-mother to
toad-son, wondering how to escape from these dreadfully strange
creatures.

The toads waited for Thumbelina to reply. When she didn't, toad-mother broke the silence, saying, "Obviously you don't have words to tell us how pleased you are! No matter, I quite understand. Keep in mind *you'll* have to work in the future. My son is used to being treated like a king and he won't abide a lazy wife. Now, I'll take this walnut bed of yours, for I have just the spot for it. But don't worry, I'll be right back to fetch you."

Toad-mother picked up the bed and set off with her son trailing close behind. Once alone, Thumbelina rushed to the edge of the lily pad, frantic to get away. Should she risk drowning rather than wait for the toads to come back? She must decide immediately, for there was no time to spare.

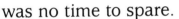

Meanwhile the fish that swam in the stream had gathered around to watch the comings and goings of the toads. Now they raised their heads above the water, hoping to catch a closer look at the little maiden. When they saw that Thumbelina was about to jump, their tender hearts went out to her.

"Excuse us, young miss," they quickly said in chorus. "Although you may think us rude, we assure you we couldn't help overhearing toad-mother's words. If you don't wish to live in the mud, perhaps we can be of some assistance. Of course, if you'd rather we minded our own business…?"

At once, Thumbelina halted and said, "Oh, please! If only you could help me to get away, I would be so grateful."

"Then we will! Give us a moment or two to do what is needed," they told her as they plunged into the stream and disappeared.

Underwater, the family of fish gathered around the stem of the lily pad. They nibbled at it with their teeth, working fast and furiously. Finally it broke apart. The lily pad upon which Thumbelina stood suddenly floated downstream, carrying her away where the toads could never find her.

"Hooray!" shouted the fish as they watched her go. "Goodbye and good luck."

Thumbelina waved and threw kisses to the fish, until she could see them no longer. Then she sat down to watch the spectacular sights as the lily pad sailed on and on, taking her far away from the land where she was born.

Soon the stream emptied into a gently flowing river, where the water shimmered like silver and brightly colored flowers grew up all along the riverbank. Birds dipped and soared across the river, singing the most lovely songs. A monarch butterfly took a fancy to Thumbelina and fluttered along beside her.

"If you happen to have a bit of string, I can use it to pull you more swiftly down the river," suggested the monarch. "You are so small that I will hardly know you're there."

Thumbelina had no string; instead she quickly untied the silk sash from around her waist. She threw one end to the butterfly, who caught it and flew on while Thumbelina held tight to the other end. Standing on the lily pad, she glided faster and faster, laughing with delight at the new adventure.

Just then a May bug came buzzing by and saw Thumbelina. Without a moment's hesitation, down swooped the insect and, fixing his claws about her waist, up he flew again, carrying Thumbelina away.

The empty lily pad floated downriver as the butterfly fluttered ahead, never suspecting that his playmate no longer held the other end of the sash.

The May bug left Thumbelina on a leaf in a tall tree and flew off. But it wasn't long before he returned with nectar from honeysuckle blossoms and offered her some. By now, Thumbelina was getting used to her peculiar adventures and she was not as frightened as she might have been. Since she was very hungry, she accepted the nectar and began to eat.

The insect was pleased with his prize and he said, "Even though you don't look at all like a May bug, I really do think you're lovely. I can't wait for all my friends to see you."

A party was arranged and every May bug within miles was invited. When they arrived, the guests looked at the tiny maiden and frowned. "Whatever does he see in *her*?" they wondered.

All the young female May bugs sat by themselves, giggling and whispering together. One said, "Pooh, she is so thin about the waist! I do think having only *two* legs would be a terrible disadvantage. Don't you agree?"

"I do indeed," replied her friend. "Why, she looks just like a miniature human being."

"And what could be more ugly!" interjected another.

Thumbelina had grown no less beautiful, but in the eyes of the May bugs she was different and therefore she must be ugly. The May bug who had carried her off heard all that was said and he soon agreed with his friends. Although he had once thought her lovely, in the end the insect wanted nothing more to do with the little maid. At last, he told Thumbelina she could go wherever she pleased, for he did not care in the least.

Down the May bug flew with Thumbelina to a field of wildflowers and deposited her, none too gently, upon a white daisy. Then he flew away without so much as a backward glance or a fare-thee-well.

Thumbelina stood watching as the insect flew out of view. She was relieved to see him go, but even so she did feel hurt by the way the silly May bugs had behaved.

"Well," she thought. "I shall live by myself in the woods where no one will bother me." And so she did.

Under a fat mushroom, she made a bed of green velvet moss, using thistledown for her pillows. When she was finished, Thumbelina had constructed a comfortable summer home all her own. Through the summer she feasted on the nectar of wildflowers as sweet as honey. When she was thirsty, she drank beads of water caught in the folds of leaves or drops of dew that hung like tears from the tips of fern. All kinds of birds—swallows and orioles, bluebirds and cardinals—sang to her. Their songs cheered her and kept her from feeling lonesome as the warm summer days passed lazily into autumn. But the signs of winter soon followed and the forest began to change.

Everywhere Thumbelina looked the vibrant colors of summer were quickly fading. The growing chill in the air caused the flowers to wither and die. The birds, who sang so sweetly to her when the sun was shining, flocked together and flew away. Icy winds blew in from the north, bringing rain, and the tiny maiden shivered under her thin summer dress that was now all in tatters. As the weeks passed, the cold rain turned to snow and each snowflake that fell upon her was like a shovelful of snow.

Thumbelina wrapped herself up in a fallen leaf for warmth, but it did no good. Her shelter had collapsed and there was no place to hide from the bitter cold. Surely the poor creature would not make it through the winter months. But Thumbelina had a brave spirit in spite of her miniature size and she was determined to manage somehow. Finally she decided, "I must move on. Perhaps with luck, I shall find a better shelter somewhere else."

Nearby a cornfield had been harvested in the fall and dry stubble was left from the rough-cut stalks. Thumbelina made her way across the field, but each step was a struggle, for an icy wind blew steadily against her. The broken stalks towered over her as she wandered through what seemed to her a grim forest of long-dead trees. Nevertheless, once she had begun, she could not turn back....there was no place else to go.

For two whole days she walked without finding food or shelter. On the third day she came upon a brightly painted yellow door at the base of an old tree stump. Beside it there was a sign that read, "Madam Field Mouse's Residence."

Cold and hungry, Thumbelina knocked at the yellow door. When the field mouse came to see who was there, Thumbelina looked like a small beggar, frail and weak. She put out both her hands and pleaded for any scraps of food that could be spared.

"Poor little maiden, why you are nearly frozen to death. Come in at once and warm yourself by my fire. I am just about to sit down to dinner and you shall join me," insisted the kind-hearted field mouse.

She fed Thumbelina corn soup and freshly baked bread until the little maiden was quite full. The field mouse would not hear of her leaving. So it was settled that in exchange for helping with the chores, Thumbelina would share her host's cozy home.

During the weeks that followed, Thumbelina kept the mouse hole tidy. She carried wood for the hearth and she gladly helped prepare the meals. Then, in the evening, the two sat together by a warm crackling fire and Thumbelina told stories to the delighted field mouse, who was quite fond of such things. This was the best part of the day and it was hard to determine who enjoyed these hours more—the teller of the tales or the listener.

During the Christmas season the field mouse told Thumbelina, "My old friend, Mr. Mole, will be visiting today. He is very wise and rich. I shall have you meet him. His home is twenty times larger than mine and he wears the most beautiful black fur coat."

Of course, the mole was enchanted by the lovely maiden and like the others before him, he decided he must make her his wife. But Thumbelina was not willing to marry the musty old mole, who spent all his time underground and never wished to see the sun.

However, the field mouse urged Thumbelina to agree, saying, "What wonderful luck! You'll have a home of your own that is bigger than anyone else's. You'll be the envy of every eligible young lady in the district."

Reluctantly, Thumbelina consented to marry the mole. If the good-hearted field mouse thought it was for the best, then she must not refuse the gentleman. So the wedding was set for autumn, the mole's favorite time of year. In the meantime, Thumbelina and the field mouse would be kept busy preparing for the wedding.

One day, the mole invited the two ladies to accompany him through a newly excavated tunnel that led directly to his own home. He went ahead carrying a torch while they followed. So it was he who first came upon a chink of daylight where the roof of the tunnel had come loose and fallen in. At his feet there lay a swallow, stiff and motionless as death.

"Don't be afraid," the mole called back to the others. "The bird is quite dead and cannot harm you."

Thumbelina was not frightened. Her heart broke to see the dead swallow lying there with its wings tightly closed and its head tucked down into its breast. "So far away from the warm sunshine," she thought. "Poor gentle bird, now you've no songs to sing."

"Horrible creatures, birds!" remarked the mole as he hurried past. "Always chirping and singing their foolish songs, as though they didn't have a care in the world. Well, this one has nothing to sing about now!"

Then and there Thumbelina vowed to come back alone to give the poor dead bird a proper burial. That night she could not sleep for thinking about the swallow. In the morning she rose up early and hurried down the tunnel, taking with her a newly made coverlet. Carefully she placed it over the bird and tucked her own pillow under his head. Then Thumbelina sat down beside the swallow and softly began a song. There surely was not another voice quite like hers, sweet as anything ever heard with a kind of magic that was clear and fresh as spring itself.

When the song was at an end, Thumbelina sighed. "I'm sure you were one of the swallows who sang to me last summer. Now neither of us can ever play in the sunshine again."

Sadly she lay her head on his feathered breast. For a moment she thought she felt the bird stir. Could it be that the swallow was not dead? Indeed, she listened again and heard his heart beat. The swallow was alive! Although he had been stiff with cold and nearly frozen to death, the warmth Thumbelina had provided was enough to revive him.

Thumbelina hurried to bring more covers and a little broth to feed the famished bird. When he was stronger, he told her his story. "In the autumn my family prepared to fly south where it's warm in the winter and the snow never falls. But I tore my wing on a thorny berry bush and I couldn't fly away with them. When the snow came it was so cold that I fell to the ground and I could not get up. That's all I remember until you rescued me."

Once he was better, the swallow prepared to leave. But Thumbelina stopped him, saying, "It's still winter outside, even though it's warm enough underground. If you leave now you'll freeze to death for sure. Stay with me a little longer till spring returns."

The swallow gratefully accepted. Thumbelina looked after him throughout the winter and they grew to be great friends.

On the first day of spring the swallow stretched his wings and readied for flight. "Come with me, Thumbelina," pleaded the swallow. "I shall put you on my back and we will fly into the green forest. We can stay there all spring and summer, and in the fall we'll fly away to the south together. Say you'll come?"

Thumbelina smiled sadly and said, "If only I could go with you. But the field mouse is planning my wedding to the mole. She has been so good to me that I cannot disappoint her by leaving like this."

"You don't want to marry that stuffy mole. By trying to please others, you've forgotten all about yourself. Please change your mind? This is not the life for you."

Thumbelina could not be persuaded. Instead, she hugged the swallow and they said their farewells. Quickly, she pulled the earth away from the roof of the tunnel. Sunshine poured down on them like a shower of golden light, bright and dazzling after the darkness of the hole.

"Goodbye, my beloved Thumbelina. I shall never forget you," said the swallow. Then he was up and out of the hole.

"Goodbye. Goodbye," Thumbelina called as she watched him fly away. When he was out of sight, she drew the earth over the top of the tunnel and the sun disappeared. In the darkness, a tear ran down her cheek. Quickly she brushed it away and hurried down the tunnel.

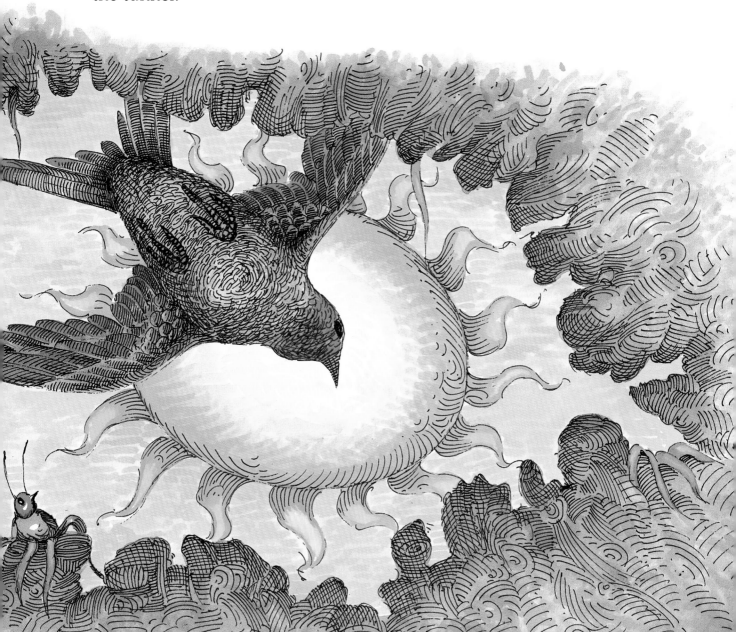

"We must begin to get your trousseau ready," said the field mouse. "Spring and summer always pass so swiftly that autumn will be here before you know it."

A half dozen spiders were hired to help weave the finest cloth for the bridal gown and veil. Then Thumbelina and the field mouse measured and cut, stitched and sewed all the garments for the new wardrobe. Each evening the mole came to visit. They all sat together and Thumbelina told stories or sang songs to please them. So long as she remembered never to mention the world above the ground, the mole was quite content. Sunshine, birds and the fresh air were all things he loathed. Clearly he didn't like hearing of things that he did not personally enjoy.

But lately Thumbelina's thoughts were often with her absent friend, the swallow, who she missed very much indeed. One night she told a tale concerning the adventures of a flock of birds. With great feeling she described their graceful flight across the sea and their songs she longed to hear again. Her desire to be among those wild creatures was all too evident to those who listened.

The field mouse hastened to change the subject, but it made no difference. The mole, who was easily upset, said good night earlier than usual that evening.

After he had gone, the field mouse scolded Thumbelina. "Oh, look what you've done. I wouldn't be surprised if the mole broke off your engagement. If you aren't careful, he will."

Thumbelina did not reply. If only she could be free without hurting anyone else, but sadly it did not seem that this was possible in a life underground.

The warm months sped by, and soon the leaves were turning yellow, then red and finally brown before they fell to the ground. Autumn with its crisp air was here and Thumbelina's wedding to the mole was only a few short weeks away. The field mouse grew more and more excited as the wedding date approached, but Thumbelina looked pale and unhappy.

One day as the two friends were out in the cornfield gathering bits of fallen corn, the field mouse asked why she seemed so sad.

Thumbelina tried to answer, but instead she began to cry.

"Dear, is it that you don't want to marry the good Mr. Mole?" Tearfully Thumbelina nodded that this was true.

"But goodness me! Why would you have said yes to the gentle-man if you didn't want to marry him?" asked the field mouse. Then she gave Thumbelina a long, thoughtful look and said, "Never mind, dear. You don't have to answer. I suppose you thought you must. But do stop crying or I'm sure you'll break my heart. You must marry whom you please or not at all and that is final."

Just then, above their heads, Thumbelina heard a familiar call. It was the swallow, flying by in the hope of seeing her one last time before he left for the winter. "Have you changed your mind, my dear little friend?" asked the swallow in midflight.

"Yes, I have!" Thumbelina called back and with that she hugged the field mouse, who hugged her back.

"Goodbye, Thumbelina. I hope you'll be happy. Don't worry about Mr. Mole. He shall find another wife. Perhaps I'll marry him myself!" said the field mouse with a laugh.

Thumbelina climbed onto the swallow's back and together they soared into the sky. Higher and higher they rose—how free she felt after the long months underground. Looking down on the world far below, every sight was a marvel to her. They passed forests and riv-ers, a vast ocean and mountain tops covered with snow. But when it grew dark and the stars came out, Thumbelina tucked her head into the swallow's soft feathers and slept.

They traveled a long distance to reach the swallow's nesting place in the south, until at last, the journey came to an end. The warm southern country was before them. But nothing the swallow had described prepared Thumbelina for such a paradise as this. Lush green grass blanketed the rolling hills, stretching on as far as she could see. Masses of wildflowers, purple and red, blue and vibrant yellow, swayed with the soft breeze that blew across the meadow-lands. Trees were laden with fruit of every kind—cherries and plums, peaches and oranges—ripening under the sun.

A shimmering white castle stood empty; its marble pillars had long ago fallen to the ground and climbing wild roses entwined the silent ruin. Year after year, for as long as the swallow could remember, his family returned to the abandoned castle to nest. Thumbelina thought it splendid, fine enough for a queen. Nearby there was a rushing brook where they drank and shouted with joy as they dunked themselves. Thumbelina laughed so hard her sides ached; she couldn't remember a time when she felt so happy.

Soon the scent of wild roses drew Thumbelina back to the castle. There the swallow left her to sit inside a pink rose as he hurried off to find his family. She breathed the fragrance and yawned with pleasure; it had been a long trip and now she was sleepy. Pulling a soft petal over herself, she settled down to rest.

When she awoke, Thumbelina opened her eyes and saw a young man, not too much bigger than herself, smiling at her from another rose. He wore a golden crown upon his head and on his shoulders a pair of gossamer wings. She thought the wings wonderful and the young man fairer than anyone she had ever seen.

"Hello," he said, when she smiled. "Are you the Rose Queen? You are so beautiful that I think you must be."

Thumbelina shook her head and laughed at the pretty compliment. "No, I'm not," she told him. "I have only just arrived from very far away."

"I am the Spirit of the Flowers. I look after each that blooms, whether rare or common; they are all in my care. For this reason my people have made me king. But surely you are one of us, no matter where you have come from," said the king.

As he spoke, a little person looked out from each rose and greeted her. They wore wings like their king and were so cheerful Thumbelina could not help but smile.

Thumbelina felt like a beggar maid standing before the king and these lovely elfin sprites. But the king leaned forward and removed his golden crown. Holding it out to her, he said, "If you'll let us, we will crown you our Rose Queen."

"It is no wonder," said the others. "Although her dress and manner is humble, she is more beautiful than a summer day."

One praised her voice, one her eyes so kind and yet so wise. In all the land there had never been such a maid as this. A tiny sprite came running and placed a pair of delicate wings upon Thumbelina's shoulders. Then they waited to hear her reply.

"Of course, I would be honored to be your queen," she said.

Oh, how they cheered and laughed and sang once she did agree. Thumbelina hardly believed her good fortune after all that had befallen her. The pushy toads, the uppity May bugs and the stuffy mole seemed so far away. Finally she had found a home where she truly belonged. Hearing the merrymaking, the swallows flew from the castle and joined the festivities with the most wonderful songs. Among them was the little swallow, so pleased and proud to see his dear friend happy at last. His song rang out above the rest—sweetest and clearest of all.